5-MINUTE SPOOKY STORIES

DISNEY PRESS

New York • Los Angeles

CONTENTS

Toy Story: Toys That Go Bump in the Night   1

Tangled: Marmalade Moon Night   15

Finding Nemo: A Fishy Terror   31

Winnie the Pooh: Boo to You, Winnie the Pooh   47

Sleeping Beauty: Maleficent Returns   63

Monsters, Inc.: Parade Day Dash   77

Peter Pan: Captain Hook's Shadow   93

Mickey & Friends: Haunted Halloween   109

Aladdin: Get in the Spirit   125

Cars: Mater and the Ghost Light   141

Beauty and the Beast: The Haunted Castle   157

Wreck-It Ralph: Tricky Treats   173

Toys That Go Bump in the Night

It was a quiet evening in Andy's room. Andy was at a sleepover, so the toys had the whole night to themselves. "What do you feel like doing?" Woody asked the others.

Suddenly, rain began pelting the windows. A streak of lightning lit up the sky.

"Reminds me of the newest Buzz Lightyear video game," Buzz said. "A storm forces me to crash-land on a hostile planet. You don't want to know what happens next."

"Yes, we do," said Bo Peep. "Telling scary stories is the perfect thing to do on a stormy night!"

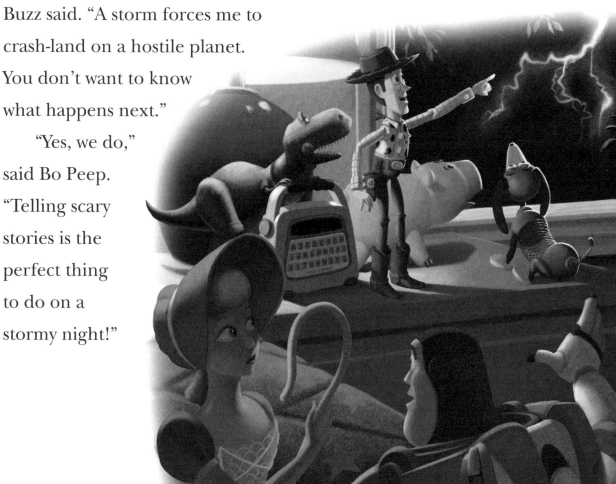

"Okay, then," said Woody. "Scary stories it is. Gather around, everybody."

"So there I am, trapped on a planet filled with angry six-headed aliens," continued Buzz. "The creatures close in on me, ready to blast me with their laser guns. But at the last minute, I activate my jet pack and blast straight up into the sky."

"Ohhhh!" said the Little Green Aliens.

"May I go next?" asked Rex.

Rex's story was about the most ferocious dinosaur ever. "He had pointy teeth and a fierce roar," Rex said. Suddenly, he roared.

"Did I scare you?" Rex asked his friends.

"Sure," Woody replied. He winked at the other toys. They all knew Rex was the *least* ferocious dinosaur around. But they didn't want to hurt his feelings.

Woody volunteered to tell the next scary story.

"Did I ever tell you guys about the time Andy and I went to a haunted house?" he asked.

The toys all shook their heads. "Well, there we were, walking in the neighborhood. Suddenly, these ghosts rose up out of the lawn! Andy ran for the front porch. But a vampire was waiting there, holding a hissing black cat."

He noticed that the other toys looked afraid. Rex had a panicked expression on his face, and Hamm was shaking so much that his coins were clinking.

"Don't worry, guys! The people who owned the house set everything up to scare the trick-or-treaters," Woody said.

"I knew that," said Rex. But Woody could see that his arms were still trembling.

"All right, gang," Woody continued, "I think we've had enough stories for tonight. Let's get some sleep. Andy will be home bright and early tomorrow morning."

Woody had just fallen asleep when he felt a nudge. He moved over a little, but then he felt another small shove.

"Woody!" Rex whispered.

"Huh?" Woody asked groggily. "What is it?"

"I heard something coming from under Andy's bed," said Rex.

"Maybe it was a noise from the storm," Woody said.

"The storm's over," said Rex.

"All right," Woody replied sleepily. "Let's have a look."

When they reached the side of the bed, Woody lifted the bedspread. "It's too dark to see anything under there," he said.

GRRRRRR!

"Good job, Rex," Woody added. "If there was anything around here, I'm sure you just scared it off."

"That wasn't me," Rex said, his voice shaky.

"It wasn't?" asked Woody. He was starting to feel a little nervous, too. "Let's get Buzz before we do any more investigating."

"This had better be an emergency," Buzz declared when
Woody shook him awake.

"I think we have an intruder," Woody whispered.

"What's going on?" asked Hamm.

"It's nothing to worry about," said Woody as calmly as he
could. "There appears to be something—or someone—under
Andy's bed."

At that moment, a rumbling came from under the bed.

"It sounds hungry!" Rex wailed. Then he fainted in fright.

The toys gathered in the center of the room while Woody
woke Rex.

Buzz strode confidently up to the bed. "This is Buzz Lightyear. You are in violation of Intergalactic Code 36920-Q, which clearly prohibits concealing oneself under another life-form's sleeping unit without prior clearance. Reveal yourself."

The only response was a high-pitched whine.

"Very well, then," Buzz replied. "You leave me no choice but to take you captive."

Buzz began to crawl under the bed. Suddenly, his space wings shot out and caught on the bedspread.

"I need some help here," Buzz called. He wriggled around, but he couldn't free himself.

"Oh, no!" cried Rex, panicking. "It's got Buzz!" Woody went to steady the dinosaur so he wouldn't faint again.

"Come on, men! We're going in!" Sarge shouted. He and the Green Army Men rushed under the bed. They freed Buzz and pulled him out.

"There's definitely something under there," Buzz told them.

"We'll take over from here," Sarge announced. "Men, we're going to execute a sneak attack!"

The soldiers split into groups and stormed under the bed.

"Halt!" boomed Sarge's voice. "It's one of our own! Switch to rescue-mission protocol!"

"Rescue mission?" Woody repeated.

"Push, men! Push!" commanded Sarge. "Now, heave-ho!"

Suddenly, RC Car shot out into the room.

"What was he doing under there?" asked Woody.

"His batteries are nearly out of juice," Sarge reported. "He just sat there spinning his wheels."

"I knew there had to be a reasonable explanation," Rex said.

Meanwhile, Buzz removed RC's battery door.

"The supply truck's coming," Sarge told Buzz. "Let's go, men!" he commanded his soldiers.

Soon RC was zipping around the room, good as new.

"Don't we feel silly?" said Hamm. "All of us so afraid, and it was only RC."

Just then, Mr. Spell lit up. "A low battery *is* scary!" he said. "In fact, I am feeling . . . a . . . bit . . . sluggish . . . myself."

"Make a note, Slinky," said Woody. "Tomorrow, fresh double-A's all around!"

Marmalade Moon Night

Rapunzel sighed. Mother Gothel was away, leaving Rapunzel alone in the tower. Luckily, her best friend, Pascal, was there to keep her company.

"What do you want to do now, Pascal?" Rapunzel asked. She'd spent the day brushing her hair (which took most of the afternoon), painting a new mural on the wall, and rereading her three books. Now it was growing dark.

She glanced over at a dozing Pascal and laughed. "No, I don't think it's bedtime yet. I'm not very tired." Rapunzel strolled to the window and gasped.

"Look at the moon, Pascal!" Rapunzel exclaimed. "It looks like a giant bowl of marmalade!"

Just then, a flock of birds flew across the night sky, making a strange face in the glowing moon.

"Ohh, that is *scary*. . . ." Rapunzel shivered with glee. Suddenly, she had an idea. "I know! Let's make tonight Marmalade Moon Night! We can start our very own spooky holiday. Now we just need some creepy traditions."

First Rapunzel wanted to make a lantern that looked like the scary moon face.

There was just one problem. There wasn't anything around the tower that was very lantern-like.

"How about . . . this?" Rapunzel asked, holding up a watermelon.

Pascal watched as Rapunzel carefully started carving.

"Ta-da!" Rapunzel said when she was finished.

Pascal looked at her carved watermelon skeptically.

"All right, all right," Rapunzel said. "It's not exactly spooky. But it's not bad for my first try."

Rapunzel put it down on the table and stepped back to admire it. As soon as she let go, the watermelon rolled off the table, hit the floor, and smashed into pieces.

"Humph," she said. "Remind me next time that moon-o'-melons tend to roll."

"Now let's play a game," Rapunzel said. She glanced at the rest of the items in the fruit bowl. "These look just like the Marmalade Moon!" she said, picking up a few peaches.

She filled a large tub with water and added the peaches, which floated to the surface.

"Okay, Pascal," she said. "Try to pick one up. But no hands—or feet! You can only use your mouth."

Pascal seemed to think it over. Then his long tongue flicked out, lassoed a peach, and plucked it out of the water.

Rapunzel laughed. "No fair!" she cried. Then she took a turn. She plunged her head into the water, mouth wide open.

She came up coughing and sputtering—without a peach.

Rapunzel tried again, and again. But each time, the peaches bobbed away and out of her reach. Finally, she climbed into the tub, standing knee-deep in the water, and tried one more time. Once again, she just could not get her teeth on a peach.

Overcome with
frustration, Rapunzel
plopped down in the
water. It sloshed over
the sides and spilled
onto the floor.

Now the peaches lay on
the floor in a shallow puddle.
Rapunzel leaned down, bit
into one, and picked it up.
"Aha!" she cried victoriously,
taking the peach out of her
mouth. "It's much easier
this way!"

While Pascal munched on his peach, Rapunzel snuck away
to put her next spooky idea into action.

"Perfect!" she said, peering into the linen cupboard.

23

A few minutes later, Rapunzel crept out of hiding by candlelight.

"Boooo! I am the Marmalade Moon ghost!" she said, whipping a bedsheet around her.

Pascal took one look at the orange figure that suddenly appeared, and panicked! His chameleon instincts kicked in and he changed color, camouflaging himself against his background.

"Boo!" Rapunzel repeated. But her friend was nowhere to be seen. "Pascal?" she called out. Realizing she might have really scared him, she added, "I'm sorry. This was supposed to be fun— not *scary*."

Where was he?

Pascal peeked around cautiously from his hiding spot. He saw Rapunzel searching under the chair. He breathed a sigh of relief as his skin slowly returned to its normal green.

When Rapunzel stood up, there was Pascal, right in front of her.

"Aaah!" she cried, and fell over backward, completely startled.

"Okay," Rapunzel admitted with a laugh, "that *was* a little more scary than fun." She sat down on the chair next to Pascal. "No more tricks," she said. "I promise."

She glanced outside and saw that another flock of birds had made a whole new shape in front of the moon. Looking at it, she had an idea for some Marmalade Moon dress-up fun *without* the spookiness. . . .

Rapunzel gathered the things she needed—black fabric, scissors, and a needle and thread—and got to work. "No peeking!" she said to Pascal. "I'm making something for you, too!"

Pascal seemed perfectly content to have a little quiet time. He had nearly dozed off when Rapunzel's voice woke him with a start. "Well? How do I look?"

She looked just like a witch—wearing a witch's hat she'd
made herself and holding an old broom. "Witches love flying
across the Marmalade Moon, especially with their little black
cats!" she explained.

"Here's *your* costume!" she exclaimed, gently tying a pair
of cat ears onto Pascal's head.

Pascal did not seem amused, but Rapunzel loved the way
both costumes had turned out. "Perfect!" she cried, clapping
her hands joyfully in front of the mirror.

Pascal cheered up when Rapunzel told him what the next part of their celebration was: eating some sweet treats. He even seemed to warm up to his costume.

So that night, high in a tower, deep in the woods, a friendly witch and her chameleon-kitty enjoyed their very first spooky holiday—together.

A Fishy Terror

It was a dark and stormy night above the sea, which meant that it was a cold and murky night beneath the sea. Nemo and his friends swam as quickly as they could. They had to find Dory—and fast!

Dory was surprised to see Nemo and his friends, but then again, with a memory as bad as Dory's, it didn't take much to surprise her.

"Hi, Harpo!" Dory said to Nemo, forgetting his name once again.

"Dory, it's me—Nemo!" the little clownfish replied.

"Hi, Nemo!" Dory said with a smile. "Have you seen Harpo?"

"Dory, we need your help," Nemo continued. "We think this part of the ocean is *haunted*!"

Nemo saw the look on Dory's face, and he knew what was coming next.

"AAAAAAAAAAAHH!" Dory shouted. She swam away from Nemo and his friends as fast as she could. If this part of the ocean was haunted, she wanted to go somewhere—anywhere—else.

"The ocean is haunted, just keep swimming, the ocean is swimming, just keep haunted . . ." she muttered. "Oh, this looks like a nice place!"

But little did Dory know she was swimming directly toward the terror from beneath the sea!

Nemo and his friends gathered their courage and swam
as fast as sailfish, the fastest fish in the seven seas. Soon they
reached Dory, who was swimming in circles.

"H-hi, Zeppo," Dory stammered as Nemo approached.

"Are you okay, Dory?" Nemo asked.

"Yes," Dory answered. "Look what I found! It's a pirate ship!"

"That's it!" Nemo's friend Ward said. "That's where the haunting is coming from. It's the terror from beneath the sea, the sunken ship of the pirate Dakkar!"

"Why is it haunted?" Nemo asked.

"Legend has it that when his ship went down, Dakkar was trapped in a cage and couldn't reach his treasure—his shiny, sparkly treasure—so he vowed to haunt the ocean until he was free," Ward said.

"Then we should let him go. . . ." a deep voice said from behind them. The fish froze, then slowly turned to see . . .

Bruce—the great white shark from Australia
with the pointy white teeth. But they didn't have to be
scared of him. Bruce had vowed never to eat fish again—
"fish are friends, not food" was his motto—so everyone
was glad that he was there. If anyone could go up against
Dakkar's ghost, it was big ol' Bruce.

"Listen, mate," Bruce said to Ward. "There's no such thing as ghosts, and I'll prove it. I'll go to that sunken ship and swim into that cage," the great white shark said. "And then you'll see that there's nothing to be afraid of."

"I wouldn't do that if I were you," Ward warned. "Everyone who goes into that cage or near that treasure disappears!"

But a spooky story about a ghost-pirate wasn't enough to scare Bruce. He led the fish to the pirate ship and got ready to swim into the cage. Still, Nemo was afraid.

"Wait," Nemo began. "If our shark goes into the cage . . . and the cage is in the ship . . . and the ghost-pirate's in the ship . . ." he said, slowly putting the pieces together.

"It's bye-bye Brucey!" Ward interjected.

"I love that song!" Dory added.

"Maybe you shouldn't go in there, Bruce," Nemo said to his friend.

"No worries, mate," Bruce said as he swam up to Nemo and Dory. "If you think this little boat is going to scare me, you're going to need a bigger boat." He gave them a reassuring smile.

"Okay, Deuce, good luck with the ghost-pirate. Hope you don't find that bigger boat!" Dory said with a wave of her fin.

And with that, Bruce the shark swam into the cage. His friends anxiously watched him go.

Bruce waited a few seconds. Nothing happened. He waited a few more moments, and then . . .

"Who dares enter the sunken ship of the dread pirate Dakkar?" a voice boomed. Bruce looked all around, but there was no one there. "You will never escape from the terror from beneath the sea!" the voice warned. It was the ghost-pirate!

As soon as Nemo and Dory heard the voice, they knew that they had to help their friend. They swam to the cage and pulled and pulled to break Bruce free, but the cage wouldn't budge. The ghost must've locked it!

"Last chance," the ghost-pirate voice yelled. "Leave my treasure ship or I will trap you all here with me forever!"

"I'll be right back, Dory!" Nemo said as he quickly swam to the top of the ship.

Something weird was going on. He could hear the ghost-pirate yelling louder there. It was almost as if it was coming from that part of the ship. Nemo slowly swam around the side of the hull and saw Ward's tail sticking out. Then he heard Ward yelling, "Beware the dread pirate Dakkar!"

It couldn't be, but it was! Ward was the ghost-pirate!

Nemo yelled
down to Bruce that the
ghost-pirate was really their
friend Ward. Bruce used his
great strength to break free of
the cage!

The gang confronted Ward,
who confessed to making everything
up. "I collect shiny things," Ward
began. "The gold coins, the jewels . . . they
all would've gone so well in my collection,"
he said. "I tried to scare everyone away so I could find
the treasure, but you guys were all too brave to scare."

"Well, this *isn't* a treasure ship, mate," Bruce said. "It's
a fishing boat. I used to eat here all the time . . . back when
I ate fish."

"But even if it was, we would've helped you look for treasure if you'd asked," Nemo said. "Friends help each other; they don't scare each other."

"I'm sorry, guys," Ward replied guiltily. Suddenly, he had an idea. "Let me give you all something from my shiny collection to make it up to you."

"Good-bye, not-haunted treasure ship!" Dory said as they all swam off, happy that the ghost-pirate wasn't real.

"Good-bye," a voice answered from the sunken ship.

Maybe it really *was* haunted. . . .

Boo to You, Winnie the Pooh

Once each year, there comes a most peculiar day. The dark grows darker. The leaves rattle on the trees. And everything is a tad spookier.

On this particular day, Winnie the Pooh was dressed like a bee, snacking on his last drop of honey.

"Oh, Halloween," he chuckled. "Though I'm not fond of tricking, I do enjoy treating."

A few minutes later, a skeleton bounced in.

"Not late, am I?" asked Tigger, for that was who the bouncer was. Behind him were two Eeyores—the real one, who was wrapped in bandages like a mummy, and Gopher, who had dressed up like Eeyore.

"Hello, Eeyore and Gopher," said Pooh.

"Dagnabbit!" said Gopher. "You know it's *me*?!" He left to find a new costume.

"C'mon, Pooh!" cried Tigger. "We'd better get a move on!"

"But first we need to get Piglet," Pooh replied.

Piglet was putting the finishing touches on his costume when he heard a Tigger-like "Boo-hoo-hoo!" coming from his entryway.

"Why, Piglet," said Pooh as his friend hurried to greet them, "where's your costume?"

"We've got to get Halloweenin'!" said Tigger.

"Oh . . . uh . . ." Piglet stammered. He didn't really want to go outside.

"While Piglet gets ready," said Pooh, "I'll try out my costume on our friends at the honey tree."

"But, Pooh—" Piglet said, following his friend.

"Perhaps it would be best," Pooh said as he started out the door, "if you didn't say my name. It might make the bees suspicious."

But the bees knew exactly what Pooh was trying to do! They began to buzz angrily.

Pooh and the others ran away from the honey tree as fast as they could.

Nearby, Rabbit inspected his pumpkin patch.

"Perfect!" he proclaimed.

Bzzzzzzzzzzz! Suddenly, Rabbit heard the bees. He looked up just in time to see Pooh, Piglet, Tigger, and Eeyore smash into his beautiful pumpkins. The bees flew away, disturbed by all the chaos.

"Of all my favorite holidays," Rabbit sighed, "Halloween isn't one!"

Soon it grew dark, and Piglet hurried home. As he got into
his costume, he realized he was just too scared to go outside.

Suddenly, there was a knock at the door.

"Who . . . who's there?" he squeaked.

"It's me . . . them . . . us!" said a Pooh-sounding voice.

"Pooh Bear?" asked Piglet. "How can I be certain it's you?
Perhaps if you say something only you would say, then I'd be
certain. How about 'I am Pooh'?"

"You are?" said a confused Pooh. "Then who am I?"

"It *is* you!" squealed Piglet, jumping out of his costume and opening the door.

"Piglet," said Pooh, "will you be joining us for Halloween?"

"I'm afraid I'm just too afraid," Piglet replied.

"That's okay," said Pooh Bear. "We won't have a Halloween. We'll have a Hallo*wasn't.*"

"Thank you, Pooh Bear," Piglet said, smiling.

Piglet and Pooh explained their plan to Eeyore and Tigger, and with that, everyone went home.

Alone once more, Piglet created lots of notes telling all the
spookables and monstery beasts to stay away. They had to know
that it was a Hallo*wasn't* at his house somehow!

Soon, a storm began to rage outside. Pooh looked out his window. "I hope Piglet isn't too frightened," he said. "I suspect that something should be done. But what?"

He tried to concentrate. "Think, think, think!" he muttered. And, to no one's greater surprise than his own, he did just that!

"Just because Piglet can't have Halloween with us," said Pooh, "there's no reason why we can't have Hallo*wasn't* with him!"

A little while later, Tigger was bouncing around when two figures opened his door.

"*Spookables!*" hollered Tigger, tripping over his tail.

The spookables removed their sheets. It was Pooh and Eeyore.

"We're on our way to Piglet's to have a Hallo*wasn't*," said Pooh. "Would you care to come? We made new costumes since the other ones were torn in the pumpkin patch."

"What are we standin' around here for?" Tigger said, snatching a sheet.

They'd almost reached Piglet's house when a tree branch snagged Pooh's bedsheet. Pooh was certain he'd been clutched by the claw of a spookable!

"Help!" shouted Pooh.

"Pooh Bear?" Piglet said, hearing Pooh's cries from inside his house.

Tigger and Eeyore, still wrapped in their ghostly bedsheets, tried to free Pooh from the branch.

"Oh, no!" Piglet cried when he saw them. "Spookables got Pooh! I must help him, Halloween or no Halloween!"

Suddenly, Piglet noticed the costume he'd made.

"I'll save you, Pooh!" he cried, putting it on.

He stumbled outside and yelled, "Boo!" as loud as he could.

Pooh, Eeyore, and Tigger looked up in horror and ran away, leaving Pooh's costume on the branch.

They ran past a startled Gopher, who was now wearing a Rabbit costume.

"Look out! Spookables!" they screamed.

Gopher looked up just as Piglet ran into him. They both went rolling after the others.

Rabbit, who had been trying to keep his remaining pumpkins dry with an umbrella, glanced up. "Not again!" he cried, just before Pooh, Tigger, Eeyore, Piglet, and Gopher collided with him.

Costumes and pumpkin pieces flew everywhere.

Finally, they untangled themselves and discovered that there was not a single spookable around.

"You saved us," Pooh told Piglet. "You're here and the spookables aren't. You must have chased them away."

"Way to go, Piglet!" exclaimed Tigger.

Piglet's friends shook his hand. "Wait half a second, Piglet," said Tigger. "You aren't dressed up as anything for Halloween!"

Piglet realized he'd lost his costume in all the excitement. Then he smiled. "Oh, but I am," he said. "I've decided to be Pooh's best and bravest friend!"

"And that," said Pooh, smiling down at Piglet, "is precisely who you are."

Maleficent Returns

One morning, Princess Aurora and her fairy godmothers, Flora, Fauna, and Merryweather, prepared the palace for a party. It was Aurora and Phillip's anniversary, and Aurora couldn't wait to celebrate it with the kingdom.

"It looks wonderful!" she told the fairies. "I think we're just about done with decorations."

"Oh, not quite!" replied Flora. "We've still got to make everything pink."

"No, no, no!" said Merryweather. "Make it blue."

Aurora laughed. "Whatever you say, my dears," she said, leaving to check on the food preparations.

Suddenly, a shadow darkened the palace. Merryweather and Flora rushed to the window.

"Why, it's a solar eclipse!" Merryweather exclaimed, watching the sun duck behind the moon.

"So it is," Flora said. "During solar eclipses, magic works in the most mysterious ways."

"And sometimes even *scary* ways," Merryweather said with a shudder.

"Oh, I wouldn't worry," Fauna replied, coming up behind them. "With Maleficent gone, we have nothing to fear."

At that very moment, the darkness from the eclipse fell over Maleficent's castle. A green light erupted from the windows, and the stone raven perched on the balcony came to life.

"Caw! Caw!" it screeched, flying inside to search for its mistress.

Before long, the raven saw the source of the green light. Maleficent's staff was glowing. The raven pecked at the glass ball with its beak until the ball cracked. Suddenly, green smoke emerged, twisting and turning until it became . . . Maleficent!

"Come, my pet!" she said to the bird. "Let us see who's here to welcome our return."

Maleficent searched her rooms and found them to be dark and empty. "It seems you are my only faithful servant," she sighed.

Maleficent used her magic staff to check on the rest of the kingdom, and saw that everyone was gathered at the palace. Prince Phillip and Princess Aurora smiled, greeting their many guests.

Maleficent's eyes flashed with anger. "It seems we have much to do here."

In the palace, the anniversary party was in full swing, and
Aurora and Phillip were exchanging their gifts.

"Oh my goodness," Aurora said as a small puppy jumped into
her arms. "He's adorable!"

"Darling, I love it!" Phillip said as Aurora handed him a
gleaming golden pendant with their portraits inside.

Everyone cheered, ready to begin a hearty feast and an evening
of dancing.

Suddenly, a loud screech interrupted the laughter and music. Green mist flooded into the room, and Maleficent suddenly appeared.

"I see I was not invited to yet another celebration," Maleficent said coolly. "Well, this will be the last!"

Maleficent raised her staff. "Fire and ice, moon and sun, turn skin and bone into cold, hard stone!" she bellowed.

The green mist surrounded Phillip, the fairies, and the guests. They instantly turned into statues. Even the new little puppy became a stone figure. Aurora cried out in horror.

"Without the company of your loved ones, you will wither like a wilted rose," Maleficent sneered, leaving the palace in one swift turn.

Tears fell from Aurora's face as she looked at Phillip and the fairies. She didn't know what to do.

At that moment, Aurora's animal friends from the forest rushed into the room. They'd been late to the anniversary party and had seen everything from the window. They tried to comfort Aurora.

"Thank you, friends. But I can't stay here. I must go to Maleficent and break the spell somehow," Aurora said.

Though her animal friends tried to stop her, Aurora ran out of the palace and toward the dark forest.

As she got closer to Maleficent's castle, black clouds formed in the sky, and thorny bushes clawed at her legs. Aurora kept running, determined to save her kingdom.

"Lonely already, my dear?" Maleficent cackled when the princess approached.

"Maleficent!" Aurora said. "I demand you lift the curse on my people."

"Well, I couldn't, even if I wanted to help you," Maleficent replied. "A spell like that cannot be reversed."

"And if you turned me to stone instead?" Aurora asked.

Maleficent was delighted. "You would do that? Spend eternity as a statue so your friends and family would live?"

"I would," Aurora replied bravely. "But you must swear that they will awaken."

"I believe that can be arranged," Maleficent said, towering over the princess and lifting her staff into the air.

Aurora closed her eyes, bracing herself for the curse. But as soon as Maleficent uttered the words, there was a flash of light and a scream. Aurora watched in shock as the evil fairy changed into her dragon form and then disappeared altogether.

Back at the palace, Prince Phillip and the others awoke.

Worried that Maleficent had taken Aurora, Phillip rushed out of the castle to find his wife.

"Wait for us!" the three fairies called as they flew behind him.

Suddenly, a familiar figure came running toward them.

"Aurora!" Phillip cried. "Are you all right? What happened?"

As Aurora explained everything, Flora smiled at her.

"Your selflessness reversed Maleficent's spell and rid the world of her once again. Remember, love is the strongest kind of magic."

The group headed back to the palace. Soon everyone knew how Maleficent had been defeated, and the kingdom cheered for their princess's bravery. They resumed the party and continued the festivities late into the night, celebrating their courageous and noble leaders, and their love for one another.

DISNEY·PIXAR
MONSTERS, INC.

Parade Day Dash

Mike Wazowski crumpled up the last piece of crêpe paper and stepped back to admire his work.

"It's perfect!" he said to his best friend, Sulley.

Sulley hopped up onto the parade float they'd been building. It was decorated with balloons and streamers and had a row of doors in the middle, just like the Scare Floor.

It was the best float Sulley had ever seen. And when he rode it the next day, he'd be doing his favorite thing—scaring!

Sulley crept behind one of the doors and threw it open. "Rrraaargh!" he roared.

Mike put on his best announcer voice: "Introducing the Grand Monster of this year's Monstropolis Day parade . . . Mr. James P. Sullivan!"

Every year, Monsters, Inc., held a parade on the day Monstropolis had been discovered. Since Sulley had collected more screams than any other Scarer that year, he'd been asked to lead the parade.

Sulley grinned. "Want to take a practice drive along the parade route?"

"Sure. Hop in!" Mike exclaimed.

It was a beautiful evening in Monstropolis. Main Street was already lined with flags, banners, and even sour-lemonade stands.

Then Mike noticed something strange. Someone was moving behind the grandstand! He took a closer look, and then shrugged. Maybe his eye was playing tricks on him.

When they'd finished driving along the parade route, they left Mike's car with the float and walked home. They wanted to be sure to get a good night's sleep.

The next afternoon, Sulley put on his tall Grand Monster hat. Mike gave him a thumbs-up, and Sulley grinned. The friends hurried off to Monsters, Inc. They were excited to get their float up and running!

In the parking lot, everyone was getting ready for the parade. Some monsters set up floats, while others carried balloons.

Mike used a hook to attach his car to Sulley's float. "She's ready to go!" He couldn't wait to start leading the parade down the street.

Sulley jumped up onto the float. But when Mike put the key in the ignition, his car wouldn't start!

"Of all days," Mike muttered, opening the hood.

As Mike checked the engine, Sulley anxiously watched the other monsters start to pull their floats out of the parking lot. The parade would be starting any minute.

"Everything okay?" asked Mr. Waternoose, the head of Monsters, Inc. "We need you at the front of the parade, Sulley."

Sulley explained that the car wasn't
working. Just then, Randall came slinking
up. "My float is working perfectly," he said
to Mr. Waternoose. "Perhaps I should lead
the parade?"

Mr. Waternoose sighed. "I suppose that
would be best. Sorry, Sulley. I'm sure you
understand."

Randall's float was covered in mirrors,
all reflecting his sneaky image. "Sorry about
your float, Sulley," he hissed. "Let me know
if you need a lift to the gas station."

That was when Sulley noticed a puddle on the ground next to Mike's car. He sniffed it. "It's gas," he said.

Mike bent down to look, and he gasped. "Randall's footprint! He emptied the tank on purpose!"

"That sneaky reptile!" Sulley exclaimed.

"We won't let him get away with this!" Mike replied. "We have to fill the tank and catch that parade!"

Mike and Sulley ran as fast as they could to get more fuel. Before long, they were racing out of Monsters, Inc. Mike steered the float alongside a marching band at the end of the parade.

"Pardon us," Sulley called. "Coming through!"

Mike honked his horn to the same beat as the giant tuba, and Sulley tipped his hat to the conductor.

"Go get 'em, Sulley!" the band leader cried.

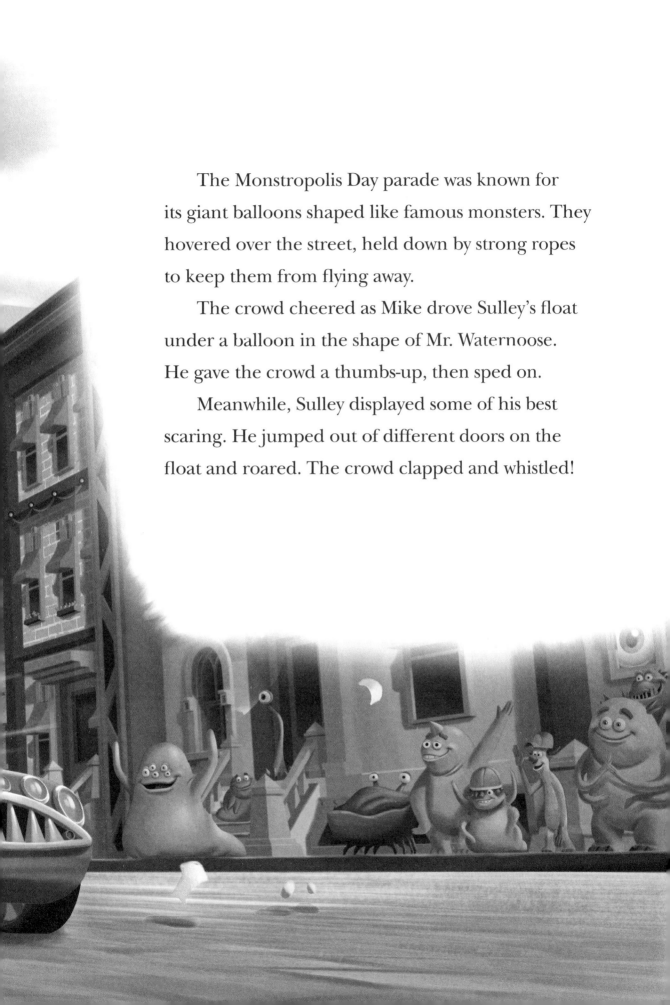

The Monstropolis Day parade was known for
its giant balloons shaped like famous monsters. They
hovered over the street, held down by strong ropes
to keep them from flying away.

The crowd cheered as Mike drove Sulley's float
under a balloon in the shape of Mr. Waternoose.
He gave the crowd a thumbs-up, then sped on.

Meanwhile, Sulley displayed some of his best
scaring. He jumped out of different doors on the
float and roared. The crowd clapped and whistled!

Mike squeezed past a float with Monster Scouts tossing gummy worms and grasshopper cookies to the crowd. The Monster Scouts squealed with delight when Sulley jumped out from one of the doors, pretending to scare them. Suddenly, Mike had an idea.

"Sulley," he called over his shoulder. "I'm going to pull up alongside Randall's float. I have an idea that will knock his socks off."

They could see Randall blowing kisses to the crowd at the front. Mike expertly wove through a line of monster-cycle riders until they were right next to Randall's float. Sulley knew just what Mike was thinking. He readied himself for the perfect moment.

"So glad you could make it after all!" Randall cackled to Mike. "Too bad you missed all the fun."

But then Sulley burst out from behind one of the doors on his float and gave Randall the scare of his life.

"RRRAAARRGH!" Sulley roared.

Randall was startled, but the crowd cheered and clapped. They thought it was part of the show!

"That was awesome!" a little monster called to Sulley as Mike drove them to the front of the parade. Sulley winked and tossed the boy his Grand Monster hat.

The crowd applauded. No Grand Monster had ever done that.

Along the way, Sulley pretended to scare the crowd, and they cheered. Sulley loved seeing everyone have such a good time!

"We hope you enjoyed the Monstropolis Day parade!" His voice echoed over the loud cheers. Then he announced, "Let the fireworks begin!"

Boom! Sparkling lights exploded in the sky, lighting up the entire town center. As everyone oohed and aahed, Sulley smiled at Mike. "Thanks, pal," he said. "You sure saved the day." Mike grinned. "Hey, what are friends for?"

Captain Hook's Shadow

"Time for you to walk the plank, Pan!" John Darling cried as he waved his wooden sword at his brother, Michael. The two boys were playing Peter Pan and Captain Hook in their nursery.

"Only if you catch me," Michael replied, "you codfish!"

Michael leaped off the bed. *Clank! Clank!* The brothers chased each other around the nursery in an exciting sword fight. For a moment, Michael felt just as he had when he was a Lost Boy in Never Land.

"All right, John and Michael, time for bed," Wendy announced as she walked into the room. She was sleeping in the nursery while her new bedroom was being decorated.

"Just a few more minutes," Michael begged. "Captain Hook is about to make me walk the plank!"

"You'll have plenty of time to walk the plank tomorrow," Wendy said.

"Five more minutes?" John asked Wendy.

"You said that five minutes ago," Wendy replied, smiling. "You can continue your battle first thing in the morning. I promise."

There really was no arguing with that, so Michael and John put down their swords and dutifully crawled into their beds, while Wendy turned out the light.

Michael pulled the covers up to his chin and snuggled against his teddy bear. He wasn't tired at all.

A few minutes later, Michael could tell by the gentle breathing sounds that John and Wendy were fast asleep. Michael squeezed his eyes shut, but it was no use. He kept picturing Captain Hook trying to capture Peter Pan—and the surprised look on the pirate's face when Peter got away!

Suddenly, there was a rattling sound, then a *WHOOSH*. Michael opened his eyes and saw that the nursery windows were wide open. Had someone gotten inside?

That was when Michael noticed a shadow against the far wall. He gasped, and his eyes widened in fright. It was shaped just like Captain Hook!

Quickly, Michael dove under the covers. Captain Hook was scary. But being under the covers didn't make Michael feel any better. He wanted to know for certain whether or not the pirate was in the nursery.

Slowly, he lifted the bottom edge of his blanket and peeked out.

Michael still couldn't see Hook, but the captain's shadow was there against the wall—large as life. The shadow seemed to look around the nursery for a moment. Then it crept toward the far corner.

A chill ran down Michael's spine.

Captain Hook was headed toward Wendy!

Michael knew he had to protect his sister. He glanced around the nursery, and his eye fell on something lying beside his bed. His wooden sword!

The littlest Darling wrapped his fingers around the sword just as the shadow got to Wendy. He threw off his covers and leaped toward it!

The shadow stumbled backward. Michael lunged at it again, but it swiped at him with its hook!

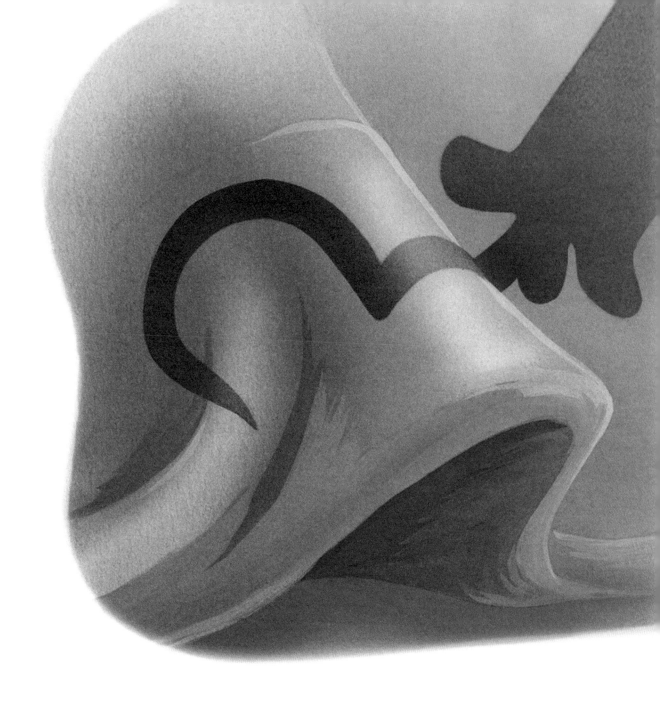

Diving under his bed, Michael scooted away just in time.

He gulped, waiting for the hook to swipe at him again.

Then he began to wonder why he was only seeing Captain Hook's shadow. Where can Hook be hiding? he asked himself.

Michael realized he couldn't stay under the bed—Hook was sure to find him there sooner or later!

Summoning all his courage, Michael darted into the middle of the room. The shadow came after him, and Michael stumbled backward, tripping over a ball that had been lying on the floor.

The shadow skulked toward him. Now Hook has got me for sure, Michael thought.

"Cock-a-doodle-doo!" a voice cried suddenly.

"Peter!" Michael exclaimed as his hero flew in through the window. "I'm so glad you're here. Captain Hook tried to get Wendy, but I stopped him."

"Hook is here?" Peter asked. He narrowed his eyes and looked around.

"Why, it's only Hook's shadow," Peter said. "Don't let it get away!" The shadow tried to run, but Peter flew after it.

"It's only a shadow?" Michael asked. Suddenly, he wasn't so scared. He leaped up and ran after it, too.

The shadow moved toward the wooden toy chest.

"Grab it from the other side!" Peter called. Michael ran toward the shadow from the right as Peter flew at it from the left.

In a flash, Michael reached out and caught it.

"Put it in here!" Peter said, holding out a sack.

Michael stuffed the shadow inside, and Peter tied the bag closed with a piece of rope.

"Whew!" Peter said. "That was close."

"Why do you think Captain Hook's shadow was here?" Michael asked.

"I stole the shadow for a prank," Peter explained. "But it's been nothing but trouble—pulling the Lost Boys's tails and putting pinecones in their beds. And then it snuck away from Never Land."

"How awful!" Michael cried.

Peter nodded. "I'd better fly back to return it while everyone aboard Captain Hook's ship is still asleep."

"Good idea," Michael said.

"Do you want to come?" Peter asked. "It'll be a great adventure!"

"I don't think I'd want to go without Wendy and John," Michael replied.

"Then let's bring them!" Peter said, flying over to Wendy's bed. He reached down to give her a gentle shake but then drew his hand back. "Aw, she's fast asleep," he said. Peter looked across the room. "John's asleep, too."

"Maybe next time," Michael said.

"Next time," Peter echoed, jumping to the window ledge.

"Good-bye, Michael. Tell Wendy and John I said hello!" he called. Then he flew off into the night.

"I will!" Michael promised. He waved and went back to bed, smiling. He was glad to have had another adventure with Peter Pan. And now he was ready to go to sleep.

Haunted Halloween

I am going to have a really terrific Halloween party tonight, Mickey Mouse thought. If I ever finish getting everything ready, that is!

He tacked a fake cobweb to the wall and looked around his living room. Jack-o'-lanterns and ghosts stared back at him.

"Everything looks nice and spooky!" he said. "I bet Minnie will love it."

Mickey glanced at the clock. "Golly!" he said. "It's almost time for the party, and I haven't put my costume together yet!"

Mickey knew he had an old pirate costume packed away in the attic. He climbed up a creaky ladder and turned on the light.

"Now where did I put that costume?" Mickey wondered.

Thunder crashed, and lightning flashed across the sky. Suddenly, the attic light went out!

"Oh, dear!" Mickey cried.

It was very dark. He stumbled into a huge cobweb . . . a real one!

"Yikes!" he said with a shudder.

Mickey tried to feel his way through the attic. After a couple of minutes, the lights came back on.

"Thank goodness," Mickey said. He spotted the old trunk he'd been looking for.

"I'll bet my pirate costume is in here." Mickey took out the key he'd brought with him. He put it in the rusty old lock, turning it easily.

Suddenly, he felt a tickle in his nose. *Ahhh-choo!* he sneezed. A cloud of dust surrounded the trunk. It looked kind of spooky as it swirled around.

"It's just the dust," Mickey said, reassuring himself. He lifted the lid of the trunk and a scary figure suddenly towered over him.

"Aaaghh!" Mickey shouted. Then he realized it was just a plastic decoration.

"Whew!" he said, relieved. "This skeleton will be perfect for my party!" He rummaged through the trunk. "There's a lot of cool stuff in here."

Meanwhile, in Mickey's backyard, Pluto chased a ball near
the clothesline full of fresh laundry. As Pluto charged after it,
one of the sheets hanging from the line came loose and fell on
top of him. It covered him from head to tail!

Just then, it began to rain. The wet sheet stuck to Pluto like
glue. He shook and shook, but the sheet stayed put. Then he
ran around the yard as fast as he could, trying to get it to fly
off. It wouldn't budge!

"Arf!" he barked in frustration.

At that moment, Donald, Goofy, Minnie, and Daisy drove up to Mickey's house. They were all dressed in their Halloween costumes.

"Gawrsh! Look at the lightning!" Goofy exclaimed.

"It sure is a spooky night," Minnie said nervously.

"Let's run right into the house," said Daisy. "If we wait for Mickey to answer the door, our costumes will get soaked."

"Mickey, we're here!" called Minnie when they entered the house. "Whcre are you?"

But Mickey didn't answer. He was still upstairs. The storm was so loud he couldn't hear his friends.

Boom! went the thunder.

Suddenly, the lights went out again.

"Uh-oh!" cried Donald.

The friends stood in the dark for a moment. *Thump-ka-thump-thump!* It sounded like something—or someone—was staggering around upstairs!

"Wh-what was that?" Daisy asked with a gasp.

"Mickey?" Minnie called.

There was no answer.

In the backyard, poor Pluto was still stuck under the sheet.

He tried to feel his way toward the doggie door.

"Aaaarrr! Arr! Arr!" Pluto howled.

"What's that sound?" Daisy whispered.

"Shh! Shhhh!" Goofy whispered back.

Just then, something white ran past the window.

"It's a g-g-ghost!" cried Daisy.

Mickey's friends were too scared to even scream!

Up in the attic, Mickey lit a candle and changed into his pirate costume. Then, picking up the skeleton decoration, he slowly and carefully headed down the dark staircase.

Mickey's friends heard a shuffling of feet and a rattling sound. They looked up to see the shadow of a horrible monster coming toward them.

"Oh, no!" Donald screamed as the others hid behind a chair.

Donald dove onto the chair and hid under a pillow. The friends prepared for the worst.

Suddenly, the lights came back on.

"Hi, everybody," Mickey said.

Mickey's friends stared at him in shock.

"Oh, Mickey, it's just you!" cried Minnie. "You really scared us!"

"We thought you were a ghost!" Goofy exclaimed.

"That's one scary costume!" Donald said with a shiver.

"Aw, I'm sorry, gang," Mickey said. "I didn't mean to scare you! I was just getting some finishing touches for the party."

Daisy picked up a cupcake and began to munch on it. "Oh, don't worry, Mickey," she said. "This is the scariest, most exciting Halloween ever! How did you do it?"

"Gawrsh, Mickey, it sure is the best haunted house I've ever been in," added Goofy.

"Er—haunted house?" said a puzzled Mickey, looking around. He had done a lot of decorating, but the house wasn't haunted. . . . At least, he didn't think it was.

Just then, Pluto found his way in through the doggie door. He happily ran into the living room. Mickey and his friends looked up and saw . . . a ghost! And, boy, did they scream this time.

"Arf!" barked Pluto.

"Oh, Pluto! It's just you!" said Mickey, relieved. "Hey, boy, you're all wet! Let's get you dried off!"

Mickey turned to his friends and grinned. "You're right. This has been the scariest Halloween ever!"

Get in the Spirit

It was a rainy day in Agrabah. Princess Jasmine stared out a window in the palace sitting room. "I wish we could go outside," she sighed.

"We can stroll around the palace," Aladdin suggested.

"Great idea," Jasmine replied. "We can go exploring!"

Nearby, Abu the monkey sat up eagerly. He'd been lounging on a pillow, trying to think of something to do.

The Genie was also bored. He'd been wandering the halls when he overheard Aladdin and Jasmine's plan.

I think it's time for a little rainy-day fun! he thought.

Aladdin and Jasmine made their way to the hallway. Abu jumped as thunder boomed and lightning flashed. Then he hopped up onto Aladdin's shoulder.

"It's just a little storm," Aladdin reassured the monkey.

After they'd walked for a while, Jasmine noticed they were in a part of the palace that she didn't recognize.

"That's odd," she said. "I don't think I've ever seen that painting before."

"Hmm . . . I think that's the shortcut to the kitchen," said Aladdin. "We could grab a snack!"

Abu bounced around excitedly. All this exploring had made him hungry.

As they continued, the air began to feel cold. Then Abu walked right into a cobweb. *"Ahhhhhh!"* he screeched.

"Are you sure this is the way to the kitchen?" Jasmine asked nervously.

Aladdin nodded. "It can't be much farther now," he said. But he didn't remember the shortcut being quite so cold or dark.

Then Aladdin saw a door with a blue arrow on it. "Aha!" he said, relieved. "That must lead to the kitchen!"

He opened the door. Suddenly, hundreds of squealing bats flew out and circled over their heads.

"Let's get out of here!" yelled Jasmine.

They ran as fast as they could down a long corridor. At the end, they saw a door. "In here!" Jasmine shouted. Once they had slammed the door, they huddled together, trying to catch their breath.

After a few minutes, the sound of the bats rustling behind the door stopped. All was still and quiet.

"*Whew!*" said Aladdin. "Glad that's over. I think this is the right way."

Aladdin led them further into the room.

"Uh . . . just a few more steps and we'll be in the kitchen making ice cream sundaes," he said.

But a few more steps led them into one of the darkest, coldest, and spookiest places they had ever been—the dungeon.

Aladdin, Jasmine, and Abu looked around anxiously. Then the sound of laughter surrounded them. Jasmine felt a shiver run down her spine.

"Even if you scream and shout, I don't think I'll let you out!" a voice boomed.

"Who are you?" Aladdin demanded. "Show yourself."

"Here I am—your lovely host. I'm the creepy dungeon ghost!" the ghost shouted as he appeared in front of them.

Aladdin and Jasmine couldn't believe their eyes. They had heard about ghosts in the dungeon, but they had never dreamed they'd meet one.

Then, just as quickly as it had appeared, the ghost disappeared! The group started desperately searching for the door. They were all turned around now.

The wind howled as Aladdin, Jasmine, and Abu made their way through the dark, twisting halls of the dungeon.

Aladdin wondered how they would ever get back upstairs.

Then the floor gave way. Suddenly, everyone went flying down a chute!

"Aaaaahhhhhh!" shouted Aladdin, Jasmine, and Abu. They landed on the floor with a thump and looked around.

The ghost appeared again.

"Welcome to the cellar. I'll be your tour guide today. Please hold questions until the end," it said with a laugh.

Aladdin and Jasmine looked at each other. This ghost didn't seem that scary after all.

"Hey, do we know you?" asked Aladdin.

"I'll say!" the ghost said, chuckling.

Jasmine turned to Aladdin and raised her eyebrows.

Aladdin looked closely at the ghost. There was something very familiar about it.

"And do you know who I am?" asked Jasmine.

"Yeah, you're Princess Jasmine—Al's girl!" the ghost answered.

"Aha!" shouted Aladdin. "Got ya!"

He smiled at Jasmine.

"You're not a ghost. You're the Genie," Jasmine said.

"Oops, caught me!" the Genie exclaimed, turning back into himself.

"That wasn't very funny, Genie," said Aladdin.

"Yeah, you really scared us," added Jasmine.

Abu chattered angrily.

"I'm sorry," said the Genie. "It was just a little rainy-day fun."

Jasmine and Aladdin couldn't help laughing. "He's right, you know?" the princess said. "We were looking for something to do, and that *was* kind of fun."

Aladdin smiled. "Hey, Genie, can you get us out of here?" he asked.

"Yes, sir," said the Genie. He turned himself into a giant flashlight so that they could make their way through the dark hallways to the kitchen.

Soon they were happily eating ice cream sundaes. "I guess I did a pretty good job of scaring up some ice cream," said the Genie.

Everyone laughed. A boring rainy day with the Genie around? Never!

Mater and the Ghost Light

Mater the tow truck liked to play pranks on his friends. *Scary* pranks were his favorite kind. One night, he snuck over to Casa Della Tires. Guido and Luigi were admiring the perfectly stacked columns of tires outside. They'd spent hours putting it all together.

All of a sudden, Mater zoomed through the columns, screaming and making a funny face. Tires flew everywhere! Guido and Luigi were so scared they jumped high into the air.

Mater burst out laughing. It seemed like a pretty good prank.

Over at Flo's V8 Café, Lightning McQueen and Sally were talking quietly.

"Gosh—it sure is a nice night," McQueen said.

"It *sure* is," Sally replied, gesturing toward the Mater-sized shape hiding behind the stack of oilcans. It looked like their friend was about to pop out at them from behind the stack.

McQueen smiled knowingly. He started to speak loudly toward the oilcans. "I sure hope Mater isn't waiting around to scare me, because I'll—"

Mater drove up right behind McQueen, screaming,
"Heeyaa!" Startled, McQueen yelped and sped out of the way.
He had not been expecting Mater to come from that direction.

"If only you moved like that on the racetrack," Doc laughed.

"Oh, buddy," Mater said to McQueen with a chuckle. "You
look like you'd just seen the Ghost Light!"

"What's the Ghost Light?" McQueen asked.

Just then, Sheriff drove up. He started telling the cars the story of the mysterious blue light that haunted Radiator Springs. "It all started on a night like tonight. A young couple was headed down this very stretch of the Mother Road when they spotted an unnatural blue glow . . . and before long, all that was left were two out-of-state license plates!"

"Don't be too scared, buddy. It ain't real," Mater whispered to McQueen.

"It is real!" shouted Sheriff. "And the one thing that angers the Ghost Light more than anything else . . . is the sound of clanking metal!"

As Sheriff told his story, Mater trembled with fear. *Rattle! Rattle! Clank! Clank!* He hoped the Ghost Light hadn't heard him. If Sheriff believed the Ghost Light was real, it had to be!

When Sheriff finished his story, the townsfolk said good night and quickly drove home. Mater was left all alone in the dark. Gulp!

The scared tow truck drove to his shack in the junkyard. He hummed a tune nervously. The Ghost Light ain't real, he thought, I'm just being silly.

Just then, a ferocious monster popped out from the shadows! Mater gasped and looked at it closer. It was just a gnarled tree, but he was trembling and shaking so much that his one good headlight fell off and broke.

Plunged into darkness, Mater hurried into his shack. Everything will be fine, he thought, trying to reassure himself.

Suddenly, a light glowed in the distance.

"AH! It's the Ghost Light!" Mater shrieked, quaking with fear.

"Ghost Light, I respect thee. Return from where you came!" he continued. He put himself in reverse and backed as far away from the light as he could.

Mater braced himself as the light flew right up to his face. All was quiet and still. He opened one eye to peek at it.

"Oh, it's just a lightnin' bug," he laughed. "And anyhow, Sheriff said the Ghost Light was blue, not yeller."

Just then, he noticed a bright blue light right behind him.

"Eyaaah!" He screamed and drove away as fast as he could, trying to lose it.

"The Ghost Light's right behind me!" Mater yelled.

He zoomed forward.

"Now it's in front of me!" He gasped, driving backward. "It's right on my tail!"

Mater raced through the tractor field so quickly that the tractors tipped over. This was not how he normally enjoyed tractor tipping!

Mater sped through all the peaks and valleys and the
canyons and craters in Radiator Springs. No matter where he
went, Mater couldn't get away from the Ghost Light.

"The Ghost Light's gonna eat me!" he cried. He was starting to get tired from all this driving. But he kept trucking along as fast as he could. He had to get back to his friends.

Finally, Mater came to a stop in front of Flo's. McQueen, Sally, and the others were there.

"Watch out!" he yelled. "The Ghost Light's comin' up right behind . . ." Mater stopped midsentence when he saw the grins on his friends's faces.

Mater looked down and saw that the Ghost Light was really just a lantern that had been hanging from his tow cable.

"Hey, wait a minute . . ." he started.

"Gotcha!" McQueen said with a laugh.

"Shoot," said Mater. "I knowed it was a joke the whole time."

"You see, son, the only thing to be scared of out here is your imagination," Sheriff told him.

"Yup. That and, of course, the screamin' banshee," added Doc.

"The screamin' what?!" Mater asked fearfully. It was time for another scary story. . . .

The Haunted Castle

"Oh, Mama!" Chip wailed as his mother, Mrs. Potts, ran the water in the sink. "Why do I have to take a bath?"

"Now, now, Chip," Mrs. Potts said as she gave Chip a good scrubbing with a sponge. "You want to look your best for your birthday tomorrow, don't you?"

"I guess so," Chip giggled. "That tickles," he said as Mrs. Potts patted him dry with a towel.

"All right, we're all done," Mrs. Potts said.

"Look, Belle!" Chip cried as Belle walked into the kitchen. "I'm clean as a whistle!"

Belle laughed. "You look very nice," she said. "Are you excited about your birthday tomorrow?"

"Am I?!" Chip cried happily. "Mama says that we'll play lots of games. Isn't that right, Mama?"

Mrs. Potts nodded. "That's right, Chip," she said.

"Do you think I'll have a birthday cake, too?" Chip
asked Belle.

"Well, I don't know," Belle said, winking at Mrs. Potts.
"I guess you'll just have to wait and see."

Chip sighed happily. The next day was going to be the
best day ever. He just knew it.

Just then, Chip yawned.

"All right, Chip, time for bed," Mrs. Potts said as she nudged him toward the china cabinet.

"But how can I sleep when I'm so excited about my birthday?" Chip asked, yawning again.

"Oh, I think you'll manage," Mrs. Potts said as she gave him a quick kiss. "Good night."

"Good night, Chip," Belle said.

"Good night," Chip said. His eyelids were very droopy. In another minute, he was fast asleep.

A few hours later, Chip woke up with a start. The kitchen was very dark. There wasn't even a crack of light coming in from the door to the hallway. Everyone must be asleep, Chip thought. He blinked sleepily.

Suddenly, he heard a long, slow creak, and then the rattle of metal. It's coming from the silverware drawer, thought Chip.

"Who's there?" Chip whispered into the darkness. But nobody answered.

Then the noise stopped. But soon it started again, more quickly this time.

Chip shivered. "Come out and show yourself!" he said, trying to be brave. He wished that there were some light in the kitchen. He couldn't see a thing.

Suddenly, the drawer closed with a bang. Then Chip heard footsteps, and the low click of the door closing.

"I better go see who it is," Chip said as he jumped out of the china cabinet. "What if it's a ghost—or a monster? I'll go warn Mama and Belle, and they'll wake the Beast." Chip was pretty sure the Beast could scare away any ghost or monster that got into the castle . . . as long as someone warned him in time. But he didn't want to wake anyone up until he was absolutely sure what they were dealing with.

Carefully, Chip climbed down from the table and hopped into the hall. Someone had forgotten to close the curtains, and the light of the moon shone into the hallway. But Chip still couldn't see very well. Suddenly, a floorboard squeaked! Chip ducked behind some draperies.

Then he heard voices.

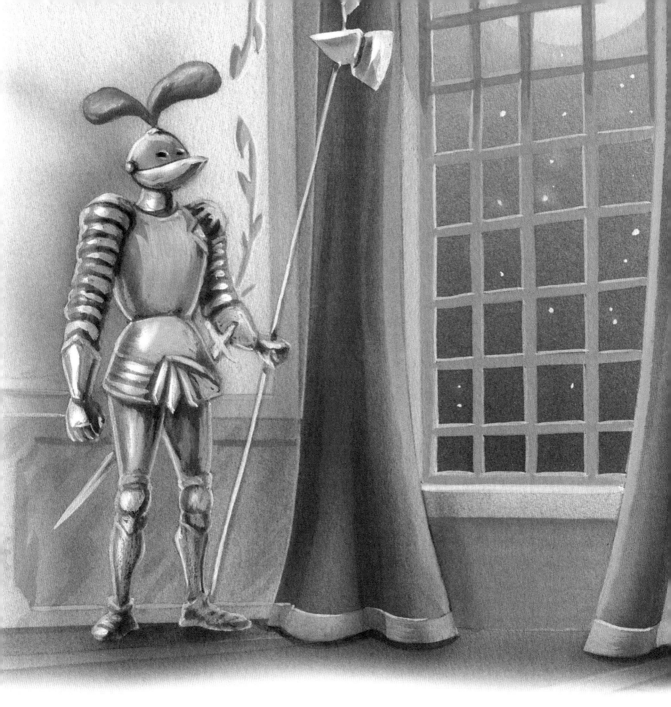

"I've got them," a voice whispered.

"Good. Let's go," another voice said.

"The others are waiting."

Others? Chip thought. Could the house be full of ghosts *and* monsters?

Chip was scared, but he knew he couldn't just stand there while the creatures were roaming about.

Sure enough, the floorboards above Chip's head let out a low squeak.

There were ghosts and monsters everywhere!

Thud, thud, thud. Some of the creatures were making their way up the stairs.

Chip peeked out from behind the curtains to see what they looked like.

But it was still too dark—Chip couldn't see very well. If he wanted to get a better look at them, he was going to have to follow them.

The little teacup hopped up the stairs quietly.

When he reached the second floor, he stopped. Along the wall, Chip saw a long shadow. It must be one of the monsters, he thought. It was enormous and had a large bumpy head and sharp claws. It was even more frightening than the Beast!

Finally, the shadow of the monster disappeared into a room.

Chip just had to see what the monsters looked like, so he decided to go in. He took a deep breath, quickly hopped to the door, and let it swing open.

When he saw what was inside, he let out a gasp!

"Chip!" Belle cried. "What are you doing up so late?"

"My heavens!" Cogsworth, the mantel clock, shouted as he dropped the large present he was carrying. "We haven't even finished decorating for your surprise breakfast birthday party yet!"

"Surprise party?" Chip asked. "You mean there are no ghosts or monsters?"

"Goodness, no," said
Lumiere, the candelabrum.

"Why were you in the
kitchen?" Chip asked.

Cogsworth held up a pair
of scissors. "We needed these from the silverware drawer,"
he explained. "To cut the streamers."

Belle laughed. "Well," she said, "I guess this really was a surprise!"

Chip grinned. He was glad that the surprise had turned out to be a party, and not a bunch of ghosts and monsters!

"Thanks, everyone," he said happily. "This is the best birthday surprise ever!"

Tricky Treats

"**H**appy Halloween, Vanellope!"

Vanellope von Schweetz looked up and grinned. "Ralph!" She jumped into her friend's large arms for a hug.

"Hey!" Ralph said. "Did you miss me?"

"Nah," Vanellope replied. She tweaked his nose, then leaped down to the ground. "Why would I miss a big, clumsy fleabag like you?"

"I dunno," Ralph replied. "Probably the same reason I missed a snarky little know-it-all like you." He ruffled her hair.

Vanellope *had* missed Ralph. Her friend spent most of his time in Fix-It Felix, Jr.—the video game where he lived. She was so happy he'd come to Sugar Rush for Gloyd's annual Halloween party.

"C'mon," Vanellope said. She grabbed Ralph's hand, dragging him toward her candy go-kart. "Let's go for a ride!"

"What about the party?" Ralph asked.

"We can be fashionably late," Vanellope replied, hopping into the driver's seat. Ralph climbed onto the back of the kart.

"Ready?" Vanellope asked. She gunned the engine.

Ralph grinned. "Ready!"

Whoosh! They were off.

"Whooo!" Vanellope whooped as they tore around a turn.
The kart skidded on two wheels for a moment.

"Gah!" Ralph yelled. He clutched the fender to keep from
falling off. Vanellope grinned. Then Ralph yelled again, and
this time he sounded *really* surprised.

"Pumpkin!" Ralph cried.

"*Pumpkin?*" Vanellope said. "What are you talking about?"

Then she looked around her. "Where are we?"

The go-kart track was gone. Ralph and Vanellope had been taken somewhere else. Somewhere *spooky*.

"I have no idea," Ralph said. "It happened when my head hit that floating pumpkin."

"Jumping jelly beans!" Vanellope yelled. She couldn't believe it! "This must be the Halloween bonus level where Boo Bratley lives! I thought it was just a myth!"

"Boo who?" Ralph asked.

But before Vanellope could make a joke about Ralph crying . . .

"WoooOOOooo!"

Vanellope and Ralph jumped a mile. A marshmallow ghost had appeared out of nowhere!

"Boo Bratley!" Vanellope exclaimed, pointing to the ghost. "The meanest, brattiest ghost in all of Sugar Rush. Legend has it he was exiled to this bonus level many Halloweens ago."

"Soooooo haaaaaappy you've heeeeard of me," Boo Bratley taunted. "Tooooo bad that won't help you goooooo hooooome."

"Hey, wait a minute!" Ralph leaped off the kart. "We need to go back."

"You neeeed to caaaaaaaatch meeeeeeee first," the ghost moaned. Then he floated straight through the graham cracker castle doors and out of sight.

"Come on!" Vanellope yelled as Ralph opened the castle doors and climbed back onto the kart.

Vanellope and Ralph zoomed into the castle. They raced past dancing licorice brooms sweeping up cotton candy cobwebs and little jack-o'-lanterns grinning at them from the windowsills. Boo Bratley flew farther and farther ahead of them.

"Bet you can't caaaaaaatch meeeeee," Boo Bratley shouted.

"We'll see about that!" Vanellope muttered under her breath.

She stomped on the gas, and they sped through the castle at lightning speed. The chase led them up marzipan ramps to the attic, down wobbly gummy-worm ladders to the dungeons, out to a candy-corn maze, and back into the castle again.

"Bet you can't caaaaaaaatch meeeeee," Boo Bratley repeated at every turn.

"*Argh*! If he says that one more time . . ." Ralph groaned.

"It's my caaaaaatchphraaaaaase," the ghost called over his shoulder.

Finally, Boo Bratley floated right through a castle wall with no doors or windows.

"Hold on, Ralph!" Vanellope yelled. She gunned the engine so they could drive up and over the chocolate stone wall.

But midway up the wall, the kart started to fall. It wasn't supposed to carry that much weight!

"Ahhhhhhhhh!" Vanellope and Ralph fell crashing to the ground.

"Tee-hee-heeeeeee!" They could hear Boo Bratley laughing from the other side. "Looks like you're not goooooinnng hooooommmmme!"

"Argh!" Ralph said, rubbing his backside. "We're *never* going to get out of here. And I've got butterscotch hay in my pants from that stupid candy-corn maze."

"I have an idea," Vanellope said. She whispered it in Ralph's ear so Boo Bratley couldn't hear.

Ralph grinned. He raised his fists and started smashing at the chocolate walls. Stones cracked and bittersweet shards flew everywhere. Soon Boo Bratley wasn't laughing anymore!

Vanellope waited for just the right moment as Ralph distracted the ghost with his wrecking. Then she closed her eyes and concentrated. *Zap!* She glitched over to the other side of the wall, where Boo was sneaking away.

"Ha!" Vanellope said. She tapped him on the shoulder. "Got you!"

"*WINNER!*"

Fireworks went off, and sirens blared. Vanellope and Ralph had beaten the Halloween bonus level!

A candy-cane doorway suddenly appeared. "Ready to go back to Sugar Rush?" Vanellope asked. Ralph nodded. But before they could walk through the doorway . . .

"Wait!"

Boo Bratley floated up to Vanellope and Ralph. "Please don't go," he said. "Won't you stay for a little while?"

Suddenly, Boo didn't look bratty anymore. Now he just looked . . . lonely. "Nobody comes to play with me here. You guys are lucky. You have a best friend." His eyes glistened with marshmallow-fluff tears.

"Hey," Ralph said. "We know what it's like to be alone."

Vanellope nodded. "We can stay for a little while."

"Wooooonderful!" Boo Bratley cried. He clapped his marshmallow hands together. "Let's play some games!"

"Oh, yeah," Vanellope said, cracking her knuckles. "You're on."

"We should be heading back," Ralph said after a while. "I think we're more than fashionably late for Gloyd's party."

"You should come with us, Boo," Vanellope suggested.

"Oh, no," Boo replied. "That's very kind of you. But I couldn't possibly leave the castle."

"Wait, I have an idea!" Vanellope responded. "We'll be right back."

A few hours later, Gloyd's Halloween party was in full swing at Boo Bratley's castle.

"I just want to say thank you to my new friends Ralph and Vanellope!" Boo Bratley announced. "This has been the best Halloween ever."